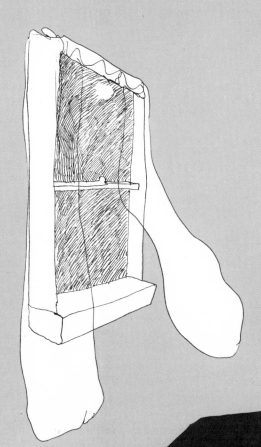

Miranda's Pilgrims

Story & Pictures by
ROSEMARY WELLS

BRADBURY PRESS
Englewood Cliffs, New Jersey

For *H. W.*
who knew the Pilgrims too

"Are you going to cry, George?" asked Miranda.
"Yes," said George, who was only four.
"I have a lion and a tiger and a skipping worm
under my bed and I can't sleep."

"But this is the middle of Kansas.
There aren't any lions
or tigers, there's only
boring old cornfields, silly,"
said Miranda.
"SKIPPING WORM!" sobbed George.

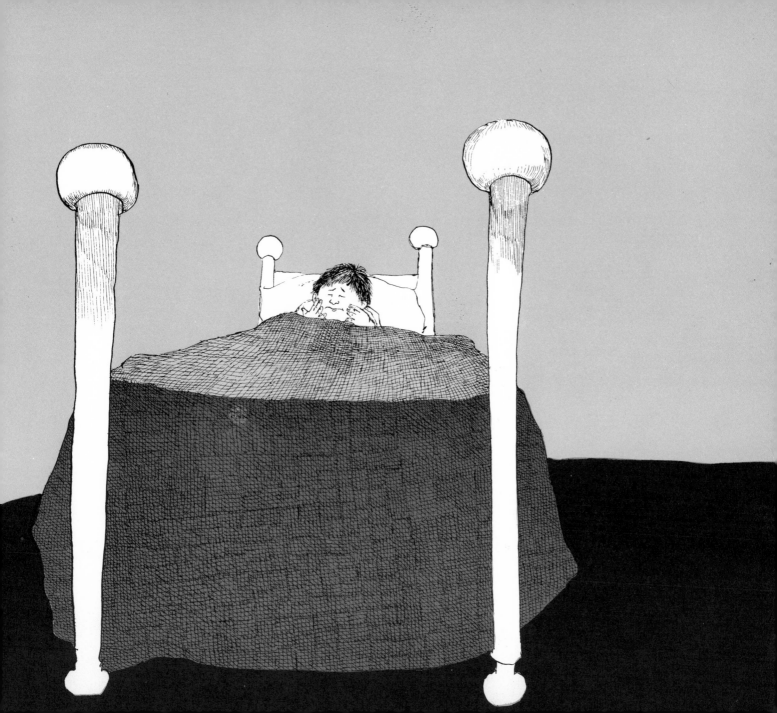

"Miranda, have you been scaring George?"
asked their mother from the doorway.
"Of course not," said Miranda.
"Then why is he crying?"
"Because he's a silly!" said Miranda.
"She *scared* me!" wailed George.

"That's not one bit true!"
said Miranda, punching George.

"When are you ever going
to learn to be good?"
said Miranda's mother,
and she sent her right to bed.

Next door,
George was very quiet.

Miranda couldn't sleep no matter how she tried.
"Thrumm, Thrumm, Thrumm." She could hear
the Pilgrims under her bed. "Oh why can't I have
something easy under my bed?" she said to herself.
"Why does it have to be Pilgrims?"

The first Pilgrim crawled out.
"I'd better say something nice,"
thought Miranda.
"I'm going to try very hard to be good
from now on," she said.
"Well," said the Pilgrim,
adjusting his hat, "in that case you
shall have to work very hard at it,
just the way we do."
"Is that what the Thrumming is?"
asked Miranda timidly.
"THRUMMING!" said the Pilgrim.
"Thrumming! That's not Thrumming,
that's the sound of good hard work!"

The Pilgrim was quickly followed by
nineteen others. "I'll never say the word
Thrumming again," Miranda promised herself.

Miranda got out of bed.
A Pilgrim turned around
and handed her a large hoe.
"Here," he said, "work."

Miranda worked.
She pushed and pulled and chonked, but no
matter how she struggled the hoe didn't
begin to make a dent, and it was heavy
and splintery and hurt her hands.

"Oh dear," Miranda sighed, "I can't
even work properly. I'll never be
any good. It hurts too much."
So she sat down.
A butterfly came to sit beside her.

STOMP!
It was gone.
"You're supposed to be working!"
said a Pilgrim.

"Lazy,"
said another.
"Besloth,"
said a third.

Miranda held the poor crushed butterfly.
"You're not good at all!" she shouted.
"You're mean!"

At this the Pilgrims shrank noticeably
and ran out under the door
without another word.
Someone was crying.
"Is that the butterfly?" Miranda wondered.

But it was only George.
"Hey," said Miranda.
"Why don't you go sleep
in my bed?
I'll take care of the lions
and tigers for tonight."

"Watch out
for the skipping worm,"
said George.

BUILDING #19 LOW PRICE

$100

33

BUILDING #1